Valley of the Eagles

Microfiction from Old New Mexico

Loretta Miles Tollefson

Some of these stories were previously published in Moreno Valley Sketches and Moreno Valley Sketches II, although they may have been subsequently revised for this collection.

While many of the events in these stories are based on rhw historical record, they are works of fiction, not biography or history. The thoughts, words, and motivations of the historical figures in this book are as much a product of the author's imagination as the descriptions, words, thoughts, and motivations of the fictional ones.

ISBN: 978-0-9983498-4-8

Palo Flechado Press, Eagle Nest, New Mexico

Other Books by Loretta Miles Tollefson

Old New Mexico Fiction
Old One Eye Pete
Not Just Any Man
The Pain and The Sorrow (Sunstone Press)

Other Fiction
The Ticket
The Streets of Seattle

Poetry
But Still My Child
Mary at the Cross, Voices from the New Testament
And Then Moses Was There, Voices from the Old Testament

A Note about Spanish Terms

Most of the stories in this collection are set in northern New Mexico and reflect as much as possible the local dialect at that time. Even today, Northern New Mexico Spanish is a unique combination of late 1500s Spanish, indigenous words from the First Peoples of the region and of Mexico, and terms that filtered in with the French and American trappers and traders. I've tried to represent the resulting mixture as faithfully as possible. My primary source of information was Rubén Cobos' excellent work, *A Dictionary of New Mexico and Southern Colorado Spanish* (University of New Mexico Press, 2003). Any errors in spelling, usage, or translation are solely my responsibility.

Table of Contents

A GOOD ARRANGEMENT

As the man on the ridge watched, the herd of elk below suddenly broke and pounded across the icy stream toward the cover of the trees. Three wolves, two grays and a black, chased after them, then slowed and sat, watching them go. A young bull elk with a limp had lagged behind the herd, and the wolves appeared to be studying him. A raven cawed overhead.

The man smiled. The wolves had identified his target for him. He reached to lift the bow from his back. It was a good arrangement, he mused as he slipped down from the ridge and began circling to get downwind of the straggling bull. When he had finished with the elk, the wolves and ravens would attack the remains.

"We will all eat well tonight," he murmured.

Which was good, because the elk herd would move more swiftly tomorrow, without the lagging one to slow them.

THE TRAPPER

The trapper studied the beaver pond carefully. Directly across the pond, on a small slick of mud, lay several short thin willow pieces, recently cut, carefully peeled. The lodge lay to his left, a four foot high mound of mud and sticks surrounded landward by a thick stand of whip-like coyote willow. Water gurgled over the dam beyond it.

The trapper slipped away from the pond and headed upstream, then waded into the icy water and back to the pond. Staying close to the bank, he moved to within a few feet of the peeled sticks. He unslung the beaver trap from his shoulder and scraped at the muck in the bottom of the pond with his foot. He positioned the trap firmly in the mud, carefully set and baited it with castoreum[1], then retreated well upstream before climbing out. He headed back to camp to dry out. Now it was just a matter of time.

~ ~ ~ ~

Sure enough, there was a beaver in the trap the next morning. But it had lunged for shore, not deeper water, so it was still alive, one hind leg clenched by the trap. The animal

---

[1] Beavers produce a concentrated substance called castoreum from their cloaca and use it to mark their territory. Trappers harvested castoreum from the beaver they killed, then used it in subsequent traps to attract other beaver.

bared its orange incisors[2] and hissed aggressively as the trapper studied it from the bank.

"You were supposed to drown, damn you," the man said. He pulled his tomahawk from his belt. The beaver lunged at him. As the trapper pulled sharply back, he slipped on the muddy bank. One buckskin-covered leg went into the water. The beaver lunged again, growling. The trapper brought the tomahawk's blunt end down hard on the back of the animal's head, and it jerked and fell lifeless into the water.

"I gotta eat, too," the trapper muttered as he hauled trap and carcass out of the water. He held it up. "A big one," he said admiringly. "A thick winter pelt, too."

---

[2] Beavers have four front teeth that they use for gnawing wood. These incisors are bright orange, very hard, and continue to grow throughout the animal's life.

WINTER STOP, MORENO VALLEY

There was no grass visible, covered as it was by three feet of snow. Clouds obscured Aqua Fria Peak, meaning there'd be more snow in the night. The lower branches of the aspens were scraped raw from the teeth of hungry deer and elk, no doubt with wolves shadowing their flanks.

The old trapper cut branches for the two pack mules and created a feeding pile. They came eagerly to investigate.

What they left would clearly indicate the passing of a stranger, but he didn't expect anyone was watching for him, anyhow. And by midday tomorrow the pile would be just another white-mounded windfall.

He added wood to the fire and pulled the buffalo robe tighter around his shoulders. He wished he had some coffee or Taos Lightning. The snow-melt water was hot enough to warm him, but something with a kick in it would feel mighty handy right about now.[3]

---

[3] Agua Fria Peak lies at the southern end of New Mexico's Moreno Valley and is the site of today's Angel Fire Ski Resort.

Taos was famous during the trapper era for a distilled wheat-based alcohol called aguardiente (literally 'water of life') or Taos Lightning. It's purported to have had quite a kick to it. Manufacturers of the drink included former trappers James Baird, Thomas 'Peg Leg' Smith, William Workman, and John Rowland.

VALLEY OF THE EAGLES

It was spring in the valley of the eagles, which meant it had been raining off and on for three weeks and the usually adobe-hard clay soil was soft enough to be dug. Once Old Bill had selected a likely spot for caching the packs of beaver fur, Pepe set to work. Old Bill stood farther up the hillside, chanting in a mixture of Osage, English, and Ute. The prayers would help keep varmints away, Bill had said. Both the two-footed and four-footed kind.

It was a good location for a cache, Pepe reflected. Tucked under the hillside pines and marked by a massive sandstone boulder that would be easy to identify when they returned. After the Taos alcalde decided that the few beaver plews they'd set aside to show him were truly Old Bill's entire winter haul, Pepe and Old Bill would slip back into the valley with a Taos merchant to turn the cached furs into coin. Then Pepe would have a nice amount to take home to his wife while Old Bill gambled his own portion away.

Pepe chuckled and paused his digging to wipe his forehead with his cotton sleeve. He was always surprised at how warm it could get in this valley, as high up in the mountains as it was.

An eagle cried overhead, then a slurry of small stones rattled past him and Old Bill came down the hillside.

"Where's the other shovel?" he demanded in his nasal twang. "We ain't got the rest of eternity!"[4]

---

[4] Both these men are historical figures. The North Carolina-born mountain man William Sherley 'Old Bill' Williams was based out of Taos from the mid-1820s until his death in early 1849. He met Jesús Ruperto Valdez Archuleta (aka Pepe) in Spring 1830 and the two of them worked together from then until Williams' death.

During the Mexican period (1821-1846), furs collected by trappers were subject to customs tariffs. Trappers were required to take their 'catch' to officials in Santa Fe and pay their fees prior to selling the furs to the merchants who would then send them east for resale. However, it was common practice for trappers to cache the majority of their take and report only a small portion for customs purposes. This is what Old Bill and Pepe are doing in this story.

WILD KNOWLEDGE

He wasn't a man to pay much attention to girl children, but this one was different. She didn't seem interested in cooking or clothes. More likely, she'd be in the canyon, fishing the Cimarron River. Her brother was the dreamy one, the one watching the fish swim instead of trying to catch them.

So the man was surprised when the girl came around the curve in the path and stopped to watch him cook the wild carrot root. He'd cut off the flowers and was slicing the root into the pot of water simmering over the fire.

"Good eating," he told her. "Back home, they say these'll make your eyes strong."

She frowned. "Not that," she said.

He was hungry. He lifted a piece to his mouth.

"No!" she said sharply.

He raised an eyebrow at her and lowered his hand.

"That isn't carrot," she said. "It's poison hemlock."[5]

---

[5] The man thinks he's cooking the root of Queen Anne's Lace, a garden plant native to the eastern United States that has an edible root. Its common name is wild carrot. However, he's actually preparing Water Hemlock, a plant widespread in the West that's closely related to Queen Anne's Lace and also tastes like carrot. It's highly poisonous.

Inevitable as Clouds

"Disaster seems as inevitable as the clouds piling over those mountains and bringing yet more rain with them," the woman said wearily. She jerked her chin toward the western horizon, where gray-lined white clouds towered above the rocky peaks.

"Rain isn't necessarily a disaster," the man said mildly. "It's water for the crops and cattle, recharge for the well."

"I haven't been out of this cabin for the last ten days," the woman complained. "By the time I'm done with the morning chores, it's raining again. You're out and about, tending the cattle, seeing to the crops. I'm in the house getting the children decent and cleaning up after them."

"The rain means you don't have to haul water to the garden," the man pointed out. "The clouds are bringing it to you."

She took a deep breath, as if gearing up for an argument, then let it out, letting the anger go with it. "I'm just feeling so cooped up," she said. "I feel like a winter-bound chicken in the hen house."

"Well, we could eat you and take you out of your misery," he teased.

She chuckled and shook her head. "I'll certainly be glad when the monsoon season is over." She looked up at him, over her shoulder. "We will get a respite from this before winter sets in, won't we?"

He chuckled, drew her to him, and silently watched the clouds moving his way.

Duck Hunting

The girl lifted her skirts away from her feet and eased toward the small brown-mottled duck on the creek bank. It was busily investigating a small marshy area where water had seeped past the bank. She wished she'd brought her bow and arrows, but she'd been sent out to collect greens, not meat.

The duck had its back to her. The girl eased forward and crouched, getting into position. Her right foot pressed the edge of her skirt into the mud, but she didn't notice.

The duck turned slightly and the girl lunged forward. As her hands touched the bird's smooth feathers, the girl's foot ground into her skirt and yanked her off balance. The duck flew off with a panicked series of quacks and the girl pitched forward into the mud.

"Hell and damnation!" she said angrily. "I hate dresses!"

She got to her feet and looked down ruefully. Her mother was not going to be happy.

RATTLED

"I don't care if you don't believe me," the old trapper said as he pushed his matted brown hair away from his eyes. He shifted the Harpers Ferry 1803 rifle impatiently. "If you're too damn smart for your own good, it ain't none of my doin'." He stroked the maple half-stock with its short barrel, looked balefully at the younger man, and half-turned to place the rifle next to his pack. The metal rib brazed to the underside of the barrel glinted in the firelight. "Thinks he's smarter'n the rest of us," the trapper muttered to the wagon master, who was sitting on his heels on the other side of the fire, smoking a carved cottonwood pipe.

"I didn't say that I disbelieved you," the young man in the black broadcloth coat said evenly. He brushed a piece of ash from his sleeve. "I simply stated that I was unaware of any unique characteristic of the 1803 that was issued to Lewis and Clark's Corps of Discovery, other than the half stock and its excellent balance." He shrugged. "My father was issued an 1803 during the 1812 conflict. He recollected it quite fondly and frequently. However, he never mentioned an unusually short barrel."

"Just 'cause your Daddy didn't say it don't mean it weren't so," the old trapper grumbled.

"That may be the case," the young man said stiffly. "I was unaware that I was contradicting you. I understood that we were merely exchanging some particularly intriguing information."

"Ten dollar words." The old man rubbed at his matted hair, unfolded himself upward without looking at the others, and stalked off into the night.

The young man in the black coat looked across the fire at the wagon master. "I didn't intend to offend him," he said uneasily.

The other man took his pipe from his mouth. "Oh, I wouldn't worry about it," he said. "Old Matt gets himself worked up like that sometimes. But he's like a garden snake, all fizz and no real fury." He glanced into the darkness. "But don't say I said so. Not where he can hear. He wants you to think he's a rattler."[6]

---

[6] The .54 caliber flintlock rifle in question had evolved from the short and stocky German Jaeger rifle and was adopted for U.S. Army use in 1803 and issued to troops during the War of 1812. It was used by many early American frontiersmen and was still being issued to Army soldiers well into the 1830s. Its half stock, short barrel, large caliber, and iron rib from tail to muzzle is thought to have influenced the design of the Plains rifle which would become a favorite of many mountain men. Historians now believe that the rifle was not, in fact, carried by the Lewis and Clark expedition.

ICY MORNING

At first, the girl thought it was snowing, the tiny flakes glimmering in the early morning sun. Then she saw they were miniscule ice crystals, floating from the cabin's cedar-shake roof and the long green needles of the ponderosas that loomed above it. Sparkling flecks of ice drifted through the air like frozen sunlight. She held her breath for a long moment, taking it in.

Then her mother opened the heavy wood-plank cabin door behind her. "It's freezing out there!" she exclaimed. "What are you doing? You'll catch your death!" The girl turned reluctantly toward the house.[7]

---

[7] The girl is experiencing diamond dust crystals, the tiniest of snow flakes. They can be smaller than the diameter of a human hair and are most often seen in the bitterly cold weather that can occur in New Mexico's Sangre de Cristos during the winter months.

BENT'S FORT

"After what you been through these last couple weeks, I'd of thought you'd be right tickled to get inside four solid walls," the old man said. He pulled off his boots and lay back on the thin pallet with its mangy once-green wool blanket.

His socks were black with grime. The stench of them in the windowless room turned Timothy's stomach.

"I'll sleep out," Timothy repeated. "I suppose I've become used to having stars over my head at night."

The teamster shrugged and stretched his arms luxuriously. "Me, I seen too many downpours," he said. "Give me a dry bed under a solid roof and I'm in heaven, for sure. All I want to finish it off is a woman." He propped himself up on one elbow, eyes bright. "You think you could do somethin' about that third item while you're out there?"

Timothy laughed. "I don't speak Indian."

"Ah, all you need is whiskey and a kiss. And you're a good lookin' cub. You probably wouldn't even need whiskey." The old man grinned toothlessly. "But you wouldn't likely bring me that kind of gift, would you now? I know I sure wouldn't if I was you. Guess I'll just hafta see what I can rustle up for myself." He sat up and reached for his boots.

Timothy chuckled and moved to the door. "Good luck with getting all three of your heavenly requirements," he said.

"Huh?" The teamster was spitting on his hands, then using the moisture to slick back his grimy hair. He stopped his grooming process and frowned. "What requirements?"

"Bed, roof, and woman," Timothy explained. "Me, I think I'll just settle for a nice quiet bed."

"Good luck." The old man chuckled. "What with those two mule trains that followed us in here this afternoon, I doubt you're gonna find a quiet spot anywhere near this ol' fort."[8]

---

[8] Bent's Fort was constructed by Charles and William Bent in 1834 in what is now the state of Colorado. The adobe fort stood on the north shore of the Arkansas River, the international boundary between the United States and Mexico. It was an important stop on the Santa Fe Trail.

The Fourth Time

She could be incandescently angry and his trip to Santa Fe and back had taken a week longer than he'd told her it would, so he braced himself as he opened the cabin door.

But his wife barely raised her head from the rocking chair by the fire. She wasn't rocking. Her shawl was clutched to her chest, her face drawn and gray under the smooth, creamy-brown skin. She glanced at him, then turned her face back to the flames, her cheeks tracked with tears.

His stomach clenched. "What is it?" he asked. "The children?"

She shook her head without looking at him. "The children are fine," she said dully. She moved a hand from the shawl and placed it on her belly. The tears started again and she looked up at him bleakly. "This is the fourth time," she said. "There will—" She closed her eyes and shook her head. "There will be no third child," she choked, and he crossed the room, knelt beside her, and wordlessly took her into his arms.

Moreno Valley Trade Fair

It's a mere mule track, the man thought as he eyed the rocky ground on the hillside ahead. A fine silt hovered in the air behind him, marking the path he and the pack horse had followed from Rayado and the Santa Fe Trail at the base of the mountains.

They'd been climbing steadily and the vinegar-scented blue green junipers had given way to taller, straighter, deeper green trees: fir and pine. The man looked at them appreciatively, glad it was June and not midwinter, when the snow that provided these trees with the moisture to live would have made the trail difficult.

He clucked at the pack horse and headed up the rocky slope. At Rayado yesterday, Jesús Abreu had told him there'd be a series of small mountain valleys before he reached the larger one. Then he was to move north, to where the Cimarron River began in a marsh on the east side of the valley. The Indians met there to trade. The traveler shook his head. It was a long way to go on the chance that they'd be there. And able to pay for the goods he had with him. He hoped this worked.

~ ~ ~ ~

A short barrel-chested Indian man stood at the edge of the encampment with his arms folded and a frown on his face, watching the man and pack horse moving slowly up the valley toward him. When the trader was close enough to speak, the man moved into the path and raised a hand.

The traveler looked at him quizzically. "You talk English?" he asked.

"You come to trade?"

"I hope to," the traveler said. "If you all have something to trade with."

"If your terms are fair." The other man's gaze moved to the horse's laden packsaddle. "You sell whisky?"

The traveler shook his head. "'Fraid not."

The other man stepped to the side of the path and gestured toward the camp behind him. "Then you are welcome."

The trader moved forward but the Indian put up a hand to stop him. "If you are found with whisky, it will not go well for you," he said flatly.

"Yes, sir," the trader said, and the glimmer of a smile crossed the two faces simultaneously.[9]

---

[9] According to local tradition, the portion of Northern New Mexico's Moreno Valley that now lies under and beside Eagle Nest Lake was once a trade fair location for the area's Native American groups.

The hamlet of Rayado lies on the eastern edge of the Cimarron mountains in what is now the Philmont Scout Ranch. Founded by Lucien B. Maxwell and Christopher 'Kit' Carson, Rayado was on land owned by Carlos Beaubien and Guadalupe Miranda as part of the land granted to them by the Mexican government in 1841. Maxwell's wife Luz and Abreu's wife Petra were Beaubien's daughters. Although Maxwell would gain control over the majority of the grant following Beaubien's death in 1864, Jesús and Petra retained ownership of a parcel outside Rayado, where Jesús would die in 1900. The chapel his wife Petra built in his memory still stands near the house where they lived.

Healing

"Lincoln is dead." The old black man's face was drained and tired. He sat down heavily in the chair beside the cabin fire. "Our President is dead."

"Your President is dead," Antonio corrected him, lifting a pot lid. "He was not my presidente."

"It has been almost twenty years since nuevomexico became part of the United States," Henry said. "How long will it take you people to adjust?"

"I will never adjust." Antonio straightened and looked at his friend. "How long will it take before the marks of slavery are truly lifted from the backs of your people?"

The old man grunted in acknowledgement and gazed into the fire.

"Suffering is a difficult thing to forget," Antonio said, more gently now. "The bruises on the mind are still there long after the skin marks have healed."

"Yes," Henry said. "Still, the bruises can heal."

"With time," Antonio acknowledged. "With much time."[10]

---

[10] New Mexico was annexed to the United States as a Territory in 1848, following its acquisition in 1846 during the Mexican-American War. President Lincoln was assassinated in April 1865.

Rotten Quartz

The three men and two mules stopped and stared up the mountainside. A fall of broken rock blocked their way.

"Well, shit!" Gus said. "How're we supposed to get to that old mine shaft with this in the way?"

Herbert pulled off his hat and fanned his week-old beard. "Maybe we can go around."

Alonzo pulled his suspenders away from his rounded belly and looked down and then up the sharply angled slope. "Mules ain't gonna like that," he said.

"Guess we're done then." Gus rubbed his jaw. "Hell, I needed that gold."

Herbert shrugged and began maneuvering the mules to face back down the mountainside.

Alonzo stared across the slope at the fractured stone. "That's rotten quartz," he said thoughtfully. He stepped onto the rocks.

"Careful there," Gus said, but Alonzo only crouched down and stretched to pluck a rust-colored piece from near the center of the rockfall. He turned it carefully. "Will you look at that," he said wonderingly.

Gus and Herbert looked at each other, then Alonzo. He grinned back at them. "Might be this is as far's we need to go." He lifted the quartz in his hand. "Looks like there's gold enough right here!"[11]

---

[11] This story is based on the 1867 discovery of what would become the Aztec Mine, on the east slopes of northern New Mexico's Baldy Mountain north of today's Ute Park. Rotten quartz is quartz stained with what looks like rust. The stain indicates the presence of gold, both in the surface rock and in formations nearby. The thirty-foot depression of rotten quartz that prospectors Tim Foley, Matthew Lynch, and Robert Doherty found on Baldy's slopes signaled the presence of a lode that would be garner $1.5 million in gold in the Aztec's first five years of operation.

DECISION POINT

Five years after the Great Rebellion had ended, Benjamin still drifted. There was nothing behind him in Georgia and nothing further west than San Francisco. Not that he wanted to go there. The California gold fields were played out.

But he needed to get out of Denver. A man could stand town life only so long, and he'd been here three months. The Colorado gold fields had collapsed, anyway. Played out before he even got here.

"I've been too late since the day I was born," he muttered as he put his whisky glass on the long wooden bar.

"I hear tell there's gold in Elizabethtown," the bartender said. He reached for Benjamin's glass and began wiping it out. He knew Benjamin's pockets were empty.

"Where's Elizabethtown?"

"New Mexico Territory. East of Taos somewheres."

Benjamin nodded and pushed himself away from the bar. "Elizabethtown," he repeated as he hitched up his trousers. "Now there's an idea."[12]

---

[12] The Denver gold rush had dwindled to a trickle by the mid1860s. Minerals would not be a major factor in Denver's history again until the 1880s silver boom. In the meantime, Elizabethtown and other mining camps in the West satisfied the need to hunt for precious metals. This influx included families. Of the 106 children under eleven living in Etown in 1870, 23 percent of them had been born in Colorado.

IMPATIENCE

"This gold. They have found it in large quantities?" The lanky teenage boy named Escubal Martinez poked a stick into the logs on the fire, moving them closer together. At the edge of the mountain valley, a coyote yipped. The Martinez clan's flock of sheep shifted uneasily in the darkness beyond the firelight.

The Prussian-born traveler from Etown grinned. "Ja," he said. "But it is hard work, the digging for gold."

Escubal's uncle Xavier grunted from the other side of the flames, where he was using a knife to carefully smooth out an uncomfortable bump on the grip of his walking staff. "Borregas y carneros." He nodded at the boy. "That is wealth."

Escubal scowled at the fire.

The traveler looked puzzled. "Carner?" he asked. "Meat is wealth?"

The boy looked up. "No, Borregas y carneros," he said. "Ewes and rams." He gestured impatiently toward the flock.

Xavier moved his staff in the firelight and ran his fingertips gently over the wood. "Carne y ropa," he said meditatively. "Meat and clothes."

"Ja," the Prussian answered. "You are correct."

Escubal scowled at the fire and the traveler smiled sympathetically. It was not easy to be young and impatient.

The boy poked at the fire again. It flared briefly, lighting the night, and the flock moved restlessly, waiting for morning.[13]

---

[13] Long before gold was discovered on Moreno Valley's Baldy Mountain, the residents of Taos and surrounding communities drove their goats, sheep, and cattle into the Sangre de Cristos each summer to fatten on the mountain pastures. The Martinez clan was still grazing their stock in the Black Lake area in the late 1870s.

HOLLOW

Lucien Maxwell, the single largest landowner in New Mexico Territory, stepped from the Middaugh Mercantile porch into early June sunlight and gazed unseeing across the green valley. On the flanks of Baldy Mountain, construction workers scurried like ants around a long wooden aqueduct-like structure. When finished, the flume it held would carry water from the headwaters of the Red River, twenty miles away, to Baldy's base. Then high pressure hoses would spray the sides of the gulches that drained the mountain, flushing out gravel and the gold the miners hoped it contained.

He himself had suggested they call the flume the Big Ditch. It was a first for New Mexico Territory. Maxwell was a major investor, likely to make a substantial return both from water sales and from men wanting to buy mining rights. Yet all he could see was the letter in his hand.

Kit Carson was dead. Kit, the companion of so many of Lucien's wilderness adventures, always so full of energy, so confident in his quiet-spoken way, with his sixth sense for trouble and how to meet it. Yes, Kit had been ill, but it was still incomprehensible that he could be gone. Lucien Maxwell gazed at the men scrambling across the hillside opposite and could feel no joy in their activity and its outcomes. It all seemed rather hollow, somehow.[14]

---

[14] Lucien Bonaparte Maxwell and Christopher 'Kit' Carson were, on the face of it, unlikely friends. Their backgrounds were quite different.

Illinois-born Maxwell was well educated and had access to considerable wealth and business connections on his French-Canadian mother's side, while Carson came from the impoverished Missouri backwoods and couldn't read or write. The two men met in the mid1830s when Maxwell was in his late teens and both were connected with Bent's Fort, on the international boundary between Mexico and the United States.

Although Carson was nine years older than Maxwell, they seem to have formed a deep bond. They hunted beaver together, fought in Kearny's California campaign, and settled their families side by side in Rayado. The news of Carson's death in Spring 1868 may have played a role in Maxwell's decision to sell the Beaubien-Miranda Land Grant which he had been acquiring so assiduously from his wife's fellow heirs since her father's death four years before. There's nothing quite like the demise of a dear friend or family member to make one reassess the track of one's own life.

Miners Gotta Eat

"Me and Joe didn't come all the way out here just to cook for white men," Frank Edwards grumbled as he slammed dirty dishes into the hotel sink. "You'd think we was still slaves in Kentucky."

"You're only eighteen," Louis the cook said. He positioned a pan of potatoes on the wooden table and picked up the pealing knife. "And what's Joe, twenty-three? You all have plenty of time."

Joe Williams came in the door with an armload of firewood. "I here tell there's a gold claim for sale in Humbug Gulch," he told Frank as he dumped the wood into the bin next to the stove. "They're askin' seventy five dollars."

Frank's hands stopped moving in the dishwater. "You reckon we got enough?"

Louis looked up from his potatoes. "You two listen to me and you listen good," he said sharply. "You go to minin' and you're gonna lose every penny you have. Miners gotta eat, even when they're so broke they're sellin' their claims. Stick to feedin' 'em and you'll do better in the long run."

Frank and Joe looked at each other and shrugged. "We don't got enough anyway," Joe said. He jerked his head sideways, toward Louis. "And the old man has a point."

"You better watch who you're calling an old man," Louis said gruffly. "And that wood box ain't full enough yet, neither. Not by a long shot."[15]

------

[15] All six of the black men listed in the 1870 Elizabethtown precinct were cooks. The data doesn't reflect why these men are all in this occupation. It could have been the result of prejudice on the part of mine owners and laborers, or a choice made by the men themselves. This story imagines one possible scenario.

FIRST DIVORCE

Augusta Meinert stood firmly in the center of the makeshift courtroom, her eyes on the judge. At thirty-seven, she was still attractive, though the stubborn tilt to her chin said she didn't often take "no" for an answer.

Judge Watts studied her. "You understand what divorce means?" He spoke slowly, as if unsure her English could withstand the strain of the concept.

Augusta's chin went up. "I understand no longer the bastard takes the money I earn." A ripple of suppressed laughter ran through the onlookers behind her. She turned and glared, and the men fell silent.

"You will be a marked woman," Judge Watts warned. "This is not Germany."

She frowned. "In Germany, he takes my money and I can do nothing." Then she smiled, her eyes twinkling. "It is why I like America."

The Judge nodded and gaveled the rough wooden planks of the table before him. "The first divorce in Colfax County, New Mexico Territory, is hereby declared final," he announced.[16]

---

[16] This story is based on the Spring 1869 First Judicial Court transcripts for Colfax County, New Mexico Territory. The first case heard in the newly formed county was a petition for divorce, which was granted to Augusta Meinert Forbes. Originally from Hanover, Germany, she was allowed to revert to her maiden name and given custody of her child, a son. The only woman listed as a business owner in the 1870 U.S. Census data for Colfax County, Meinert owned and operated the Moreno Hotel in

Elizabethtown, which appears to have been used at least occasionally for court business.

CALLING THE JURY

Judge Palen flattened his palms against the rough wooden table that served as the Judicial Court bench in Elizabethtown, New Mexico Territory, and scowled at Sheriff Andrew Calhoun. "Are you telling me that you called twenty-one men for jury duty and only seven showed up?"

Calhoun was a big man, but he fingered the broad brimmed hat in his hands like a schoolboy. "Yes, sir."

"Well, go get fourteen more."

The Sheriff nodded, turned, and crossed the creaking wooden floor.

Palen turned his attention to his seven potential jury members. "All right," he said. "Now how many of you are going to have good excuses for not fulfilling your civic duty?"

Three of them sheepishly raised their hands. Palen nodded at his court clerk to begin taking their excuses and closed his eyes. And he'd thought this appointment as Chief Justice of New Mexico Territory and Judge of its First Judicial District was a logical step up from postmaster of Hudson, New York. He suppressed a sigh. How he missed the broad sweep of the river, the bustle of the town's port. He grimaced and opened his eyes. Only four jurymen left. Damn this town, anyway. The whole of New Mexico Territory, for that matter.[17]

---

[17] This story is based on the Spring 1870 First Judicial Court transcripts for Colfax County, New Mexico Territory. Because it was the county seat, court was held in Elizabethtown, where the Judge used rented facilities, since sessions convened only twice a year. One of the first tasks at each session was to appoint grand and petit juries. The Grand Jury would consider indictments and the Petit Jury would provide a pool of men to sit on cases.

Although potential members were notified in advance, usually very few appeared, and it was standard procedure for the presiding Judge to order the local Sheriff to bring in more prospective jurors. However, this process didn't normally take six 'round ups' over three days, as it did at the beginning of the Spring 1870 session in Elizabethtown.

Former Palmyra, New York, Postmaster Joseph Palen was appointed Chief Justice of New Mexico's Territorial Supreme Court in early 1869. In that role, he also served as Judge of the First Judicial District, which included Colfax County. The difference between Palmyra and Elizabethtown must have been quite a shock.

PRODUCTIVE REVENGE

Placido Sandoval slammed the pick mattock into the rocks at his feet in a blind fury. "This Prussian, this not truly americano, how dare he speak to me in such a way? As if I were dirt, less than nothing!" he fumed. "Mi familia has lived in this country for generations. I am of the conquistadors, the flower of españa, while he is of the peasants in his country. I heard him bragging of it, how he has raised himself above his ascendientes." He smashed the wide edge of his mattock against the largest of the rocks. A chip flew off, ricocheting into the face of the man working beside him.

"¡A redo vaya!" the other laborer said. "The devil! Be careful!"

Placido swung the pick again, just as sharply, and his companion stopped his own work to turn away. "It does no good to be angry," he said over his shoulder.

Sandoval glared at him. "It is good for my soul," he growled. He slammed the pick against the nearest rock. Three large pieces broke free and tumbled farther down the stone-filled gully. "I will not be beaten by such as he. I will not be cowed."

"You there!" Edward Bergmann, the mining supervisor, called from the bank above them. "You Mexicans!"

The two men paused and looked up. The Prussian's finger pointed accusingly at Placido, his fierce black eyes indignant. "Did I not tell you to go slowly, to be more methodical in your approach? I will fine you again if you do not cease that flailing around!"

"I'll flail you!" Placido muttered as he and his companion returned to their work. But his mattock chopped more sullenly now, reflecting the pattern Bergmann had set for it. Suddenly, gold glinted from the ground. Placido glanced up at the bank. Bergmann had disappeared. Placido bent swiftly and pocketed the chip of rock and ore.

Placido's companion chuckled as he continued to swing his own tool. "That is surely a more productive approach," he said. He glanced toward the bank. "Though more dangerous if you are caught."

Placido Sandoval grunted an unwilling acknowledgement as he continued with his work, chopping steadily at the inert stones.[18]

---

[18] This story is set at the Aztec Mine on the east slopes of Baldy Mountain. The mine was co-owned by Lucien B. Maxwell, who owned the land; Matthew Lynch, one of the men who'd discovered the gold there; Elizabethtown-to-Cimarron stagecoach operator V.S. Shelby; and Edward Bergmann, who also acted as the Aztec's superintendent.

A small dark-haired man with strong opinions, the Prussia-born Bergmann had arrived in New Mexico as a private in the Seventh U.S. Infantry and risen to the rank of Colonel of the New Mexico Volunteers during the Civil War. During this service, he engaged in a prolonged dispute with Captain Charles Deus, a dispute that ended in a court of inquiry and Deus's court-martial.

MISNOMER

"Who you callin' squirt?" The tall young man with the long sun-bleached hair moved toward him down the bar, broad shoulders tense under his heavy flannel shirt.

"I didn't mean anything," the man said apologetically. The premature wrinkles in his face were creased with dirt. Clearly a local pit miner. He gestured toward the tables. "I heard them callin' you that. Thought it was your name."

"Only my oldest friends call me that," the young man said.

"Sorry about that," the other man said. He stuck out his hand. "Name's Pete. They call me Gold Dust Pete, because that's all I've come up with so far."

They shook. "I'm Alfred," the younger man said. "My grandfather called me Squirt. It kind of got passed down as a joke when I started getting my growth on."

Pete chuckled. "I can see why it was funny," he said. "Have a drink?"[19]

---

[19] A pit miner dug into the earth for gold but did not tunnel in deep enough to require that space be shored up with timbers.

Inheritance

In the middle of the night, the baby began wailing frantically.

"¡A redo vaya! Good heavens!" Ramona said, sitting up in bed. As she slipped from the blankets, Carlos grunted but didn't open his eyes. Ramona paused to look down at him. She shook her head. How a man could sleep through that much crying was beyond her comprehension. He must be very tired from the digging he did for the Baldy Mountain miners every day.

As she crossed the room to the baby, she rubbed her ears with her fingers. The Spring wind was howling, which always made them uncomfortable.

She lifted Carlito from his blankets and opened her nightdress. He began suckling eagerly, whimpering a little as he did so, and rubbing his free hand against the side of his head.

So his ears were uncomfortable, too. She looked down at him as she walked the floor, and sighed. He had a lifetime of discomfort before him and there was nothing she could do about it.

EDWARD AND AUGUSTA

Edward H. Bergmann was a man whose habit of command had been reinforced by his rise from private to Lt. Colonel during the War Between the States and even if Augusta Sever had not wanted to marry him, she wasn't sure she would have had the courage to deny his request for her hand. Now, on this sunny Tuesday morning in December, she stood before her father, who as Elizabethtown's Justice of the Peace could both marry and give her away, and took a deep breath to steady her nerves. She placed her hand tentatively on Edward's sleeve. He moved his arm slightly inward and she remembered that the uniform required no touching while he wore it.

She dropped her hand and joined it to the other, grasping the small bunch of geraniums her mother had plucked from the window pot as they'd left the house. They were the only flowers available in Etown in December. Augusta lifted her head, moving away from their metallic odor. She was marrying a Superintendent of Mines, she reminded herself. They would not remain in Etown forever. She would have hothouse flowers year round, if she wanted them.[20]

---

[20] Bergmann's work as superintending partner of the profitable Aztec Mine and his investments in other operations were so successful that he was worth $60,000 in real estate by the summer of 1870 and probably more than that when he married Etown belle Augusta Sever that December. Oddly, Bergmann's real estate holdings had diminished to a mere $1,500 by April 1875, when the Territorial property tax assessment was made. However, he'd apparently made some powerful friends,

---

because when the New Mexico Territorial Penitentiary opened in Santa Fe in August 1885, Bergmann was named its first warden. If, as this story imagines, Augusta really did want to escape Elizabethtown for a more refined existence, she would have obtained her objective with that move.

SNOW

Patricia stood in the cabin doorway and looked west, across the valley. The Sangre de Cristo peaks were obscured by thick gray clouds and a white haze drifted down their lower flanks. A cold damp wind snapped against her face. There would be snow before nightfall, more by tomorrow.

"Winter is definitely here," she muttered as she headed toward the barnyard.

The chickens were already in their coop. She lifted the skim of ice from their water pan, filled the grain container, and latched the flap down over their entry door.

The horses and cow were huddled on the east side of the barn. She threw open the door and they crowded in. She ensured they had feed, then took the grain shovel back to the cabin with her, in preparation for tomorrow's path-clearing.

"All I need now is some assurance that my husband is safe and dry," she muttered as she bolted the cabin door behind her. "Wherever he is."

~ ~ ~ ~

Peter studied the icy river beyond his mule's twitching ears. "I should've started back yesterday," he muttered. The mule stirred restlessly and he reached to soothe her. The Cimarron was almost frozen over and the canyon sides above it were white with snow. Man and mule turned to look west, where the canyon climbed toward home and the Moreno

Valley. The wind gusted straight into their faces, carrying snowflakes heavy with moisture from a lead-gray sky.

The snow was coming down fast. They'd have a rough time getting through to the valley. The marsh where the river formed up would be half frozen and nasty. The mule snorted irritably and Peter nodded. "Yeah, I guess we're gonna have to wait this one out," he said.

He dismounted and led the animal out of the wind, into the shelter of a massive sandstone boulder. "Hope Patricia's all settled in," he muttered. He looked upward and shook his head. "Should of started back yesterday."

~ ~ ~ ~

After an icy night huddled against his mule in the lee of the boulder, it took Peter another two days of slogging up Cimarron Canyon before he reached the valley above.

He had to lead the mule through the most treacherous part of the marsh at the top. "Come'n now," he coaxed. "Can't you smell the cabin smoke?" But she just rolled her eyes at him.

Finally they were through, his water-soaked boots heavy on his feet, the ten inches of snow on the ground making them colder. He turned south and the mule's pace quickened.

"Smellin' home?" Peter asked sardonically. They were close enough now to make out the cabin at the base of the rise. Smoke steamed from the chimney and the figure of a woman showed at the door, one hand to her forehead, gazing in his direction. Peter's own pace quickened, in spite of the heavy boots.

THE TIRED DOG

The red-bearded man in the tattered coat and dirty blue bandana for a hat squatted in the middle of the adobe casita's single room and grunted with pleasure as he scooped the thick stew into his mouth with his fingers. The woman placed a small wooden plate piled high with tortillas beside him. The man sucked his fingers clean, then grabbed a tortilla and used it to shovel more food into his mouth.

The two children perched on the adobe banco in the corner stared silently at the strange americano until their mother motioned at them to go outside. She replenished the man's stew, then followed them.

The girl gestured toward the house and wrinkled her nose. "Come como perro amarrado," she said. "He eats like a tired dog. So rapidly and with no manners."

Her mother turned from the woodpile, her arms full. "He is our guest," she said reprovingly. "Come, bring more wood for the fire."

When they reentered the house, the man had finished his meal.

"More?" the woman asked.

He shook his head. "No, but I thankee. That's the first meal I've had in three days." He cocked an eyebrow at her. "I'm lookin' for the wife of Juan Leyba, the one that went to Elizabethtown two years ago to find work."

The woman went still, her lips stiff with fear. She licked them nervously. "I am the wife of Juan Leyba, the one who went to that Elizabethtown to labor in the mines there." She swallowed hard. "He is well?"

"Oh yes, ma'am!" the americano said. "I'm sorry to frighten you, ma'am." He pulled a small leather bag from a pocket and held it out. "This here's from him. There's about two ounces of gold in it. He says to use it to buy that land you wanted, or come to him, whichever seems best to you."

As the woman reached for the bag, the man looked at the children and grinned. He shoved his hand into another pocket. "And he sent these for the young ones. Got a little linty in my pocket, but I think they're all right." His fingers opened, revealing a collection of hard candies, enough to keep a careful man going for at least a day and a half.[21]

---

[21] A man named Juan L. Leyba, age 34, worked as a laborer in the Elizabethtown area in the summer of 1870. There are no other Leybas listed in the 1870 Etown Census and Leyba appears to have been sharing a house with three other men. Adult men in Etown outnumbered women by about 4 to 1. This story assumes that Leyba had family elsewhere and sent money home to them by whatever trustworthy means was available to him.

THICKER'N SNOT

"It's s'posed to be August, dadburn it." Julius Fairfield looked gloomily out the door of the long narrow log cabin that served as the Quartz Mill and Lode Mining Company barracks outside of Elizabethtown. "This fog is thicker'n snot."

In one of the iron beds lining the walls behind him, somebody sneezed. "And there's the snot for ye," Edward Kelly, the company's lone Irishman, chortled as he added more wood to the potbelly stove halfway down the room.

A door opened at the far end and the chief engineer came out. He ignored the men in the beds as he walked down the room to peer over Fairfield's shoulder. "That fog'll lift shortly," he said. He clapped Fairfield on the back. "Be thankful it's not rain."

"That was yesterday's gift to us all," Fairfield said gloomily. He shook his head. "And here I thought New Mexico Territory'd be drier than New York." He grinned and glanced at the engineer. "When'd you say payday was?"
Behind them, Kelly began to sing a song praising Ireland and its green hills, and a chorus of voices yowled at him to be still. The engineer chuckled and turned. "That's enough now!" he said.[22]

---

[22] Although this incident is fictional, all the men in it did work for the Quartz Mill and Lode Company outside Elizabethtown, New Mexico in July 1870. In fact, the U.S. Census data reported twenty-three men at the

company. All except Kelly were born in the United States, although their origins ranged from New York to Missouri.

ELEGANCE IN ETOWN

The men in Seligman's Mercantile watched silently as the young woman in the long pale blue silk skirts swept out of the store.

"She's a lardy dardy little thing, isn't she now?" Charles Idle, the expatriate Englishman, asked. He shook his head and stretched his feet closer to the wood stove. "That dress and hat."

Joseph Kinsinger spat a stream of tobacco toward the empty lard can by the stove. "Those silks ain't gonna last long in this mud. And the wind'll take that hat."

His brother Peter grinned. "You're just worried Desi's gonna see her and want a getup just like it," he said.

"I wonder where's she's staying," Idle said thoughtfully. "Hey Jim, where'd she say to deliver that sterling brush and comb set?"

The clerk hesitated, then shrugged. It would be all over town soon enough anyway. "The Moreno Hotel," he said.

There was a short silence, then Idle said, "Well, I guess I'd better go see how my mine's doing this morning," and rose from his chair.

"I'll bet," Peter said sardonically, but Idle only smiled and went out.[23]

---

[23] In 1870, the Seligman family's Santa Fe and Bernalillo mercantile business included a branch in Elizabethtown, New Mexico, possibly at the corner of First and Broadway, where Adolph Seligman owned

property. While this story is a work of fiction, all of the men in it are listed in the Summer 1870 U.S. Census data for Elizabethtown.

Buzzard Brains

"He ain't got the brains God gave a buzzard," the old man grumbled. He picked up his mattock and glared at the black-hatted figure retreating down the bottom of Humbug Gulch toward Elizabethtown. Then he looked uphill, toward Baldy Peak. "Idiot can't even figure out there's a storm up there and this gully likely to wash out inside another half hour."

He sniffed disdainfully and went back to work, breaking rock on the gully's southern lip, searching for the gold that was bound to be there if a man worked the stones long enough.

The young man in the black bowler hat chewed thoughtfully on his lower lip as he trudged down the center of the gulch through the gravel and broken rock. He'd offered every dollar he had for the claim, but the miner clearly wasn't interested in selling. He shook his head. There must be other options.

Halfway down the gulch, he paused to catch his breath and gaze at the mountain above. That dark cloud spoke rain. Given the southeast position of the cloud and the angle of the gulch, it was unlikely that particular cloudburst would wet this particular arroyo. However, just to be on the safe side, he moved halfway up the gully's north slope before he continued his downward trek.

The sun was glaringly bright on the dry rocks. The young man sat down on a large sandstone boulder and took off his hat. He brushed at the dust on the black felt and shook his head. He needed to find something lighter weight and less apt to show dust. He'd keep wearing this in the meantime, though. If nothing else, it protected him from sunstroke.

He glanced down at the shadowed side of his rocky seat and grinned. Like this boulder was protecting that bit of grass, growing among the pitiless rocks where no plant had a right to be.

Then his eyes narrowed and he leaned forward. He shaded the clump of grass with his hat and peered at it and the rocks around it. Then he straightened abruptly, glanced up the gully where the miner had gone back to work, and slid off the boulder. He crouched beside it and gently pried a piece of broken quartz out of the ground. He turned it slowly back and forth, examining every facet and seam.

Five minutes later, the young man sat back on his heels and turned the rock again, just to be certain. He picked up a stick and poked around a bit in the ground beside him. Then he nodded thoughtfully, stood, and looked carefully at the gulch's rocky slopes for any sign of possession. But this piece of land clearly hadn't been claimed. Apparently, no one had thought there was gold this far down Humbug Gulch.

The young man chuckled, tucked the piece of quartz into his pocket, clapped his dusty black hat on his head, and headed into Elizabethtown to file the necessary paperwork for his claim.[24]

---

[24] Humbug Gulch is located on the western slope of New Mexico's Baldy Mountain directly across from Elizabethtown.

SOFT WOOD

Samuel stroked the narrow piece of old cottonwood thoughtfully, absorbing its smoothness. It called out to be carved.

He was one of only a handful of boys living in Elizabethtown, New Mexico Territory, in this year of 1871. Almost all the other children were girls. Even worse, he was the only boy in a house full of overly particular and opinionated sisters. Samuel scowled at the wood and dug his dirty fingernail into it, cutting a rough zigzag. It felt good to mark up something that they couldn't complain about, even if he did have to hide behind the woodshed to do it, and didn't have a knife to cut it proper-like.

"What are you doing?" a young female voice inquired.

Samuel looked up warily. A girl with long honey-brown curls and large gray eyes stood at the corner of the shed, staring at the wood in Samuel's hands. She moved closer, her eyes still on the old stick. "How'd you mark it like that?" she asked. "All the wood around this town is too twisted and tough to cut into."

"This here's cottonwood," he said. "It's softer than the pine and other stuff hereabouts."

"Where'd you get it?"

He stiffened, remembering he was talking to a girl, one who was bound to boss him around. "What's it to you?" he asked.

"Well, never mind," she said. She shoved her hands into her pinafore pockets and turned to go, her head down. Her curls covered her face.

"I'm sorry," Samuel said contritely. He flung the stick away.

The girl crossed the yard to the piece of wood and bent to pick it up. She ran her fingers down the side he hadn't marked. "It's very soft," she said.

"I have a lot of sisters and they're always bossing me," Samuel said apologetically.

The girl lifted her head and grinned. "I only have one brother, but he's always bossing me."

"What'd you want to know about the wood for?"

"I want to learn how to carve," she said. "My brother knows but he won't teach me. He says carving's only for boys. I was going to try to teach myself but I couldn't find anything soft enough."

"I found that stick in our woodpile," Samuel said. "There's more in there but I'll have to dig through the stack in order to get at it."

"When you do find some, could I have a piece?"

"Sure. Why not?" He looked at her thoughtfully. "You have a knife?"

She smiled triumphantly and pulled a penknife from her pinafore pocket. They grinned at each other. Then she stuck out her hand, ready to shake. "I'm Charlotte," she said.[25]

---

[25] While these children are fictional, and Samuel's assessment of the proportion of boys to girls (almost all of the children are female!) is

skewed by his home life, this story does reflect the high ratio of girls to boys in Etown in 1871. The 1870 census data reported 76 girls under 15 and only 41 boys. There were no boys reported between the ages of 10 and 14, so there very well could have been no male playmates his age.

ATTITUDES

"Rues? Your last name is Roo-ess?" The young white man sitting at the Elizabethtown restaurant table looked at the old black man quizzically. "You mean Ruiz? Roo-eez? You got some Spanish in you?"

The cook shook his head. "All I know is what my mama told me," he said. "My daddy was a Frenchman visiting 'round in Alabama. He stayed at the Big House for three weeks and took a shine to my mama while he was there. When I was born, she gave me his last name."

"Your master let her do that?"

The black man studied the plate of food in his hands for a long minute. "After the war, we could choose what last name we wanted," he said quietly. "I chose my daddy's name."

"That food sure looks good," the white man said. He moved his knife and fork farther apart on the bare wooden table.

Louis Rues put the plate down and turned away. He shook his head. People are people, no matter where you go, he thought ruefully as he went back to his stove.[26]

---

[26] The biographical information Louis Rues provides to his inquisitive customer in this story is imagined, but the man himself is not. In 1870, Alabama-born Louis Rues was working as a cook in Elizabethtown, the occupation of all six of the black men in the precinct. He was 45 years old.

THE LOST SOUL

As Jorgé Ruibal wandered up the middle of the road toward Elizabethtown proper, the men outside the taberna watched him sympathetically. "El joven es como alma en pena," Carlos Otero, the Etown jeweler, said. "The young man is like a lost soul."

"Si," said the boy's uncle. "He has lost his laborer job with Señor Bergmann. His papá is very angry with him."

"I heard he was in love and that his love was unrequited," Eduardo Suaso, the taberna's musician, said.

María de la Luz, the boy's cousin, appeared from around the corner of the building. She carried a basket of clean linens for delivery to Henri Lambert's Etown restaurant and hotel. She gazed at Jorgé, who'd stopped to poke his foot at a stone in the road. "He wants to leave here, but his papá is unwilling," she said.

Jorgé, oblivious to these explanations, stood in the dusty street and poked at the stone with his boot. The piece of rock was so inert and yet so full of a kind of compressed energy. He looked east, toward the massive bulk of Baldy Mountain. The gullies that swung out from its sides were full of stones and men scrambling through them looking for gold. Yet the mountain bulked there impassively, impervious to the miners who crawled over it.

Jorgé crammed his hands in his pockets and stared upward, drinking in the mountain's stony greenness, its lack of engagement with the tiny men poking at its skin.

At the taberna, the americano miner called Hobart Mitchell came out the door with a drink in his hand and considered the staring boy. "He looks like an idiot, standing there," Mitchell said indignantly. "Touched in the head."

The others all nodded noncommittally and continued to gaze sympathetically after Jorgé as he wandered on up the road.[27]

----

[27] All of the people named in this story, with the exception of María de la Luz, are listed in the July 1870 Etown census data. New Mexico-born Jorgé Ruibal was 19 years old and living with his laborer father and five siblings. Carlos Otero, born in Mexico, worked as a jeweler, while the 28-year-old Mexico-born Eduardo Suaso was a musician. Hobart Mitchell, at 38 the oldest of those present, was born in New York. Although he is listed in the census as a gold miner, he reported no assets. This incident and the motivations and descriptions of the characters involved in it are, of course, fictional.

THIS HORRID WIND

The boy woke in the night to wind howling through the rafters and down the rock-and-mortar chimney. The chimney stack passed through the cabin loft and the boy's sleeping pallet lay next to one end of the stack. He reached to touch it. The stones were icy cold. The boy grimaced. The morning fire would take an extra long time to light. The kindling itself would be cold. He scrunched farther into the blankets, seeking his own warmth.

At the other end of the chimney, his sister stirred. "Is that wind?" she asked sleepily.

"Banshees," he said.

She made a chuckling sound and he grinned, more awake now, and suddenly cheerful. "Elk on the roof, bugling," he said.

"Wolves at the door," she suggested.

"Wolves in the fireplace."

"Werewolves howling."

"La llorona weeping for her children."

The wind gusted sharply. The cabin shuddered, then a sustained high-pitched howl whistled through the roof overhang outside.

"La llorona screeching for her children!" the girl giggled, trying to stifle her voice, and then the boy was laughing too, not so quietly.

The wind dropped abruptly and there was a rustle of movement at the base of the ladder. "What in tarnation are you two doing up there?" their father called softly from below. "Your mother is trying to sleep."

"But not succeeding," their mother's voice said. Lamplight flared from below. "You two might as well come on down," she said. "This horrid wind is keeping us all awake."[28]

---

[28] The cautionary tale of la llorona is still used in New Mexico to frighten children into staying home at night, and to stay away from bodies of water. Legend has it that la llorona was a woman who drowned her children (the reasons for her actions vary depending on the version of the story). She now haunts the night wailing and searching for her dead babies. She'll drown any child she runs across, especially those who wander too close to acequia ditches or other dangerous bodies of water.

A HALF BROKE CHESTNUT

Jerry was sitting on the top rail of the corral fence, twirling his lariat thoughtfully and studying the horses, when Betty came out of the house.

She scattered the grain to the chickens and crossed the yard to the corral.

"I don't suppose you'd want a half broke gelding for a birthday present," he said, nodding toward a chestnut-colored pony.

Betty chuckled. "Not 'til you break him."

"He's right pretty."

"He is. And half broke."

He grinned. "You chicken?"

"Just smart. Married you, didn't I?"

He smiled down at her as he unbuttoned his right shirt pocket with his left hand.

"How 'bout this instead?" He handed her a small plush-covered box.

"Oh, Jerry," she said. She opened the box. Two small diamond chips on a heart-shaped locket gleamed up at her in the sunlight.

"Oh, Jerry," she said again as he slipped down to give her a kiss.

HARVEST

Alison straightened and put her gloved fists on her hips, rotating her shoulders up and back to release the ache in her muscles. Ten two-hundred-foot rows of potato plants stretched before her. She twisted around to look behind her and stretch her muscles at the same time. She had dug up the potatoes from about half a row. Full bushel baskets between the plants marked her progress. She shook her head. The yield was good this year, but her back was tired already.

She looked up at the turquoise blue sky. There were no clouds at the moment, except for a small gathering over Cimarron Canyon. An east wind was starting up, which meant rain at some point this afternoon or evening.

Alison turned in a slow circle, studying the mountain tops. Snow dusted Baldy to the northeast and Wheeler Peak to the west. She went back to her digging. She didn't have much time.[29]

---

[29] Farming in the Moreno Valley may have begun prior to the 1867 founding of Elizabethtown. Local tradition says Wilford Witt established a homestead six miles south of the future town site in 1860. Local farmers continued to produce cash and barter crops well into the 20th century, growing peas, carrots, onions, cabbage, lettuce, potatoes, barley, wheat, and oats.

MOUNTAIN VALLEY COW PUNCHING

Harry nudged the cow pony with his heels and she trotted out to edge the spotted cow and its calf back into the bunch moving downhill toward Moreno Creek. While the pony did her work, Harry turned his attention to the trees topping the rise on his left. He'd been through them once already, but he had a suspicion he'd missed something. Then he saw it. A massive black bull rose slowly from a hollow in the ground, gazed at the herd below, then turned and headed toward the top of the hill and the trees.

Harry sighed. "Collect 'em all," Gallagher had said. "Even the bastards."

The cow and calf were now meandering alongside the rest of the herd, which continued its downward trek.

Harry turned his pony's head toward the rise. The bull was nowhere to be seen. Harry shook his head. Damnedest thing, herding cows up here. Too many trees entirely. When he got his month's pay, he was headin' to Cimarron, maybe beyond. Out on the plains, where people knew how to ranch. No more mountain valley cowpunching for him.[30]

---

[30] Beef cattle were introduced to the Moreno Valley about the same time that Elizabethtown was founded in 1867 and continue to be raised there today. This cowboy's employer is John Gallagher, an Irish immigrant who started as a laborer in Elizabethtown and soon branched into ranching in what is now the Eagle Nest area.

Too Silent

The boy sat silently near the creek bank and watched his twelve-week-old puppy among the grasses, sniffing invisible trails. The boy had learned from long practice to sit motionless for long stretches of time. Being still enabled him to see much that other humans, especially adults, would never discover—coyote puppies learning to hunt, damsel fly nymphs emerging from their chrysalis, the way a brook eddies at times against the wind.

The dog might never see these things either, the boy reflected complacently as he watched his new pet. Not until he was much older and had learned to be still.

In the warm mountain sun, the boy's shoulders relaxed and his eyes began to glaze over. He wasn't prepared for the sudden movement from above. The golden eagle's outstretched wings shadowed the boy and dog at the same moment, then the pup gave a high-pitched yelp and was gone, the boy too startled to cry out.

When he stumbled home with a tear-streaked face, his mother folded him wordlessly into her arms. "I sat too still," he moaned into her chest. "I was too silent!"[31]

---

[31] Golden eagles are present in New Mexico year round and in the mountains during the warmer months. They're thirty to forty inches from beak to tail and their wings can span as much as seven feet. They have no trouble taking prey such as a large jack rabbit—or a twelve week old puppy.

SLICK

The rain was behind him and gaining fast.

Timothy looked back, down the valley, and kicked at the mule, but it was hot and the mule had been going for a long time. Its pace quickened for a few yards, then dropped back into an easy trot.

The boy groaned and looked back again. His mother had told him to take his slicker, but he'd been in a hurry. "C'mon, Boss," he begged, but the mule just flicked its ears and jogged onward.

Somehow, they made it to the barn before the clouds reached them. Timothy turned the mule into the stall and made a dash for the house. The first raindrops bit into the dust as he reached the steps.

His mother opened the door. "Get wet?" she asked meaningfully.

He grinned at her. "Dry as a bone!" he said.

DARKER THAN A WOLF'S MOUTH

"No, don't go out there now," María said. "It is late and there is no moon. El es oscuro como boca de lobo."

"How d'you know how dark it is inside a wolf's mouth?" Alvin Little grumbled as he put on his boots. "Leave me be."

He paused again, listening. The sound came again, the rattle of sticks tumbling off the pile of kindling just outside the door. "I spent two hours yesterday cutting that kindling and I'm damned if someone's gonna go stealing it."

"El noche es más mala que Judas," she protested. "It is unsafe."

He reached for the door latch, then turned to look at her. "More evil than who? Judas, you say? Where d'you get this stuff?"

He stopped on the sill and shook his head as he peered into the darkness. A pale sliver of moon and no starlight. Heavy clouds blanketing the sky. He chuckled. So this was what a wolf's mouth looked like.

He leaned forward and peered at the wood piled alongside the cabin. He could just see the once neatly stacked kindling. Sticks lay haphazardly at the foot of the pile, as if someone had tried to climb it. Alvin scowled and stepped into the yard to gather them up.

A slight scratching sound came from the shake-covered roof, but Alvin didn't have time to do more than lift his head before the mountain lion was on top of him, or hear more than María's single scream before the big cat's teeth found his throat.[32]

---

[32] While mountain lions, also known as cougars, catamounts, or pumas, are more likely to attack a deer, small woman, or child than a grown man, they do hunt at night and are unpredictable. At 130 pounds, an adult male cougar is certainly capable of taking down a man, especially one on the ground beneath its perch.

An August Morning

The old woman woke to a crisp but balmy August day, the kind that can only be experienced in the Sangre de Cristo mountains. She smiled as she threw back the cabin's shutters. Sunlight and fresh air flooded in. The sky was a clear blue. In the west, a small white cloud lifted off the tip of Wheeler Peak.

She heard the whispery flutter of wings as a juvenile bluebird settled on the porch rail opposite the window. The bird tilted its head back and opened its beak, then looked around with a puzzled air. Where was its mother?

A juvenile sparrow flew in and settled a few feet away. It pecked at the rail, looking for bugs, then gave up and flew off. The young bluebird chirped helplessly, but still its mother didn't come.

The old woman chuckled and the bird startled and flew off. The woman took a deep breath of fresh air. There was work to be done in the cabin, but still she stood there, soaking in the light.

She chuckled again, this time at herself. "You would think I've never seen an August morning before," she muttered. "Yo contento como una niña con zapatos nuevos. I am as happy as a child with a new pair of shoes."

She chuckled again and turned into the cabin, hurrying to complete her morning chores so she could go outside and play in the sunshine.

TRAPPER IN LOVE

"I had me a little señorita once," the old trapper said. "She was a real firecracker, that one. I never did learn Spanish real good and she could pull herself up all royal-like and tighter'n a beaver trap all set to snap and not near as useful. She'd start spittin' Spanish at me like some kinda wildcat and I didn't know what she was sayin' but I knew enough to let her be 'til she got over her fuss. She'd push her black hair away from her fire-flashin' eyes and let out with 'Es más feo que un dolor de estómago!' and then she'd yell 'Es más sabio que Salomón!' I didn't know a word o' what she was sayin' but I could tell from her tone that it was high time to skedaddle on outa there and go huntin'."

The old man shook his head. "Guess I went huntin' one too many times, 'cause one day I come back with a nice big cougar pelt and she was done gone. Too bad. That was the prettiest skin I ever saw."

He leaned forward. "What's that you say? I was uglier'n a stomach ache and thought I was smarter'n King Solomon? That's all she was sayin'? Here I was sure she was ready t' take a knife t' me or send her brother Sol t' do it for her. An' all she was doin' was grumblin'? Hah! Well, if I'd of known that I mighta stuck around more and tried lovin' her back into some kinda reason. She sure sounded god awful unreasonable at the time."

The old man sat back, clicked his tongue against his teeth, and shook his head. "Huh, " he said. "You don't say."

FISHING

Almost as soon as he woke that morning, he decided to go fishing. There were chores to do, sure, but the sky was slightly overcast, and the breeze was light and cool on his skin when he stepped onto the cabin's porch. Good fishing weather.

He let the chickens out of their pen and gathered the eggs, then cut himself some bread. The cow hadn't calved yet, so there was no butter, but that was all right.

He collected his pole and headed to the Cimarron. As he settled onto his heels just below the first set of beaver ponds, he heard the swoosh of wings overhead. He looked up. A bald eagle was settling itself onto a snag at the head of the pool. A heron stood in the water below, apparently ignoring both eagle and man.

"Why in tarnation would any man want to live in a town?" the fisherman wondered.

SOURCE LIST

Cobos, Rúben. *A Dictionary of New Mexico and Southern Colorado Spanish.* Santa Fe: Museum of NM Press, 2003.

Dodson, Carolyn, and William W. Dunmire. *Mountain Wildflowers of the Southern Rockies.* Albuquerque: UNM Press, 2007.

Favour, Alpheus. *Old Bill Williams, mountain man.* Norman: U of Oklahoma Press, 1962.

Meketa, Jacqueline Dorgan. *Louis Felsenthal, citizen-soldier of Territorial New Mexico.* Albuquerque: UNM Press, 1982.

Freiberger, Harriet. *Lucien Maxwell, villain or visionary.* Santa Fe: Sunstone Press, 1999.

Montano, Mary. *Tradiciones Nuevomexicanas, Hispano arts and culture of New Mexico.* Albuquerque: UNM Press, 2001.

Moreno Valley Writers Guild. *Lure, Lore, and Legends of the Moreno Valley.* Angel Fire: Columbine Books, 1997.

Russell, Carl P. *Firearms, Traps, and Tools of the Mountain Men.* New York: Skyhorse Publishing, 2010.

Stanley, F. *The Elizabethtown (New Mexico) Story.* Dumas: Stanley, 1961.

Tekiela, Stan. *Birds of New Mexico.* Cambridge: Adventure Publications, 2004.

1st District Court Transcript, Colfax County, New Mexico Territory, Spring 1869 through Fall 1870.

1870 U.S. Census records. http://www.usgenweb/census/nm/
colfax/1870/, accessed Spring 2015.
Colfax County Real Estate Transaction records. Colfax
County Clerk, New Mexico.